ETERNAL EMBER

Seraphina Blake

GLOBAL
PUBLISHING
SOLUTIONS

ETERNAL EMBER by Seraphina Blake
Published by Global Publishing Solutions, LLC
923 Fieldside Drive
Matteson, Illinois 60443
www.globalpublishingsolutions.com

This book or parts thereof may not be reproduced in any form, stored in a retrieval system, or transmitted in any form by any means—electronic, mechanical, photocopy, recording, or otherwise—without prior permission of the publisher, except as provided by United States of America copyright law.

Copyright © 2024 by Seraphina Blake

All rights reserved.

International Standard Book Number:
9798330294305
E-book International Standard Book Number:
9798330294312

Unless otherwise indicated, all the names, characters, businesses, places, events, and incidents in this book are either the product of the author's imagination or used in a fictitious manner. Any resemblance to actual persons, living or dead, or actual events is purely coincidental.

Printed in the United States of America

TABLE OF CONTENTS

Ember's Sanctuary 1
The Discovery 5
The Map 9
Into the Forest 13
The Guardian of the Woods 17
The Clearing 21
Echoes in Code 25
The Revelation 28
The Call to Adventure 32
The Trials 36
The Convergence 39
Reflections 42

EMBER'S SANCTUARY

In the quaint town of Eldoria, nestled amidst rolling hills and ancient forests, Ember Holloway's life revolves around her beloved bookstore, "Whispers of Eldoria." With eyes that hold the wisdom of ages and a gentle demeanor, Ember is the heart and soul of the shop—a sanctuary where every book seems to exhale stories untold. Each day begins with Ember unlocking the heavy oak door, greeted by sunlight filtering through stained-glass windows depicting myths and legends. Among shelves lined with centuries of human knowledge, she feels a deep connection to the stories within, seeing each book as a portal to unseen worlds.

Ember's love for books is not just a passion but a lifelong affair rooted in her childhood, where she would spend hours tucked away in corners of libraries, her imagination ignited by tales of adventure, mystery, and magic. The bookstore itself, a haven of knowledge and wonder, reflects her eclectic taste—ancient tomes on alchemy and mythology sit alongside contemporary novels and philosophical treatises. The scent of old parchment mingles with the aroma of freshly brewed tea, creating an atmosphere that draws scholars, dreamers, and seekers of wisdom alike.

Her attic apartment above the bookstore is a haven adorned with maps, tapestries of mythical creatures, and curious artifacts—a retreat where Ember finds solace and inspiration among ancient manuscripts illuminated by candlelight. The walls tell stories of their own—maps of far-off lands where dragons soar and seas teem with merfolk, tapestries that depict battles between gods and mortals, and shelves that groan under the weight of forgotten treasures waiting to be discovered anew.

THE DISCOVERY

One fateful afternoon, while rearranging a section of historical tomes in the dimly lit corner of her bookstore, Ember's fingers brushed against an unusually large and weathered volume tucked away behind rows of smaller books. Its cover, bound in cracked leather and embossed with intricate patterns that seemed to shift in the flickering light, bore no title or author's name. Curiosity sparked, Ember carefully slid the heavy book from its place, feeling a strange tingling sensation as she did so.

The tome itself was surprisingly light in her hands, its pages yellowed with age and edged with a delicate filigree of gold. She hesitated for a moment, captivated by the mysterious aura emanating from its worn surface, before gently opening it. Inside, the parchment was thick and textured, each page adorned with elaborate illustrations that danced with a life of their own. Symbols and runes, unfamiliar yet strangely compelling, adorned the margins like guardians of hidden knowledge waiting to be deciphered.

Ember's heart quickened as she turned the pages, each revealing a new chapter in a story that seemed both ancient and timeless. The ink, a deep shade of midnight blue that shimmered in the candlelight, held secrets whispered across centuries. Here were tales of lost civilizations and forgotten realms, of heroes and heroines whose names had faded from memory but whose deeds had shaped the very fabric of history. It was as if the book itself were alive, its pages resonating with a power that transcended mere words.

The discovery of this mysterious tome marked a turning point in Ember's life, awakening a thirst for knowledge and adventure she had long suppressed. As she delved deeper into its pages, she found herself drawn into a journey that would lead her beyond the confines of Eldoria, into realms where ancient prophecies and hidden truths awaited her keen intellect and brave heart.

THE MAP

Deep within the heart of the ancient tome, nestled between chapters that spoke of realms cloaked in mist and cities carved from living stone, Ember discovered a folded parchment. Its edges were frayed with age, the ink faded to a soft sepia hue that spoke of journeys undertaken long ago. Unfolding it carefully, she found herself gazing upon a map unlike any she had seen before.

The map depicted a landscape that mirrored the terrain surrounding Eldoria, yet its borders extended far beyond the familiar boundaries of the town. A network of winding rivers and dense forests sprawled across the parchment, marked with symbols that glimmered faintly as if touched by moonlight. At its center, nestled within the embrace of towering mountains and veiled in mist, lay a destination marked only by a single word: Destiny.

Ember traced the path with her fingertips, following the lines that meandered through valleys lush with verdant foliage and across plains where wildflowers bloomed in a riot of colors. There was a sense of purpose woven into the map's intricate lines, a journey waiting to be undertaken that promised revelations beyond imagination. As she studied the ancient parchment, a whisper of wind brushed against her cheek, carrying with it a faint echo of voices long since silenced.

This map, she realized, was not just a guide to physical landscapes but a key to unlocking the mysteries woven into the fabric of the enchanted realms. It spoke of ancient pacts and prophecies, of guardians and challenges that awaited her along the path to her destiny. With the map in hand, Ember knew that her journey had only just begun, and the discoveries that lay ahead would redefine her understanding of the world and her place within it.

INTO THE FOREST

That evening, beneath a sky painted with hues of twilight, Ember found herself standing at the edge of the forest, the map clutched tightly in her hand. The air around her seemed to hum with a quiet anticipation, as if the ancient trees themselves were whispering tales of forgotten magic and untold destinies. The forest loomed before her; its depths veiled in shadows that danced with the flickering light of fireflies.

With each step into the heart of the woodland, Ember felt the weight of her ordinary life in Eldoria fall away, replaced by a sense of wonder and curiosity that pulsed like a heartbeat within her chest. The forest welcomed her with a tapestry of sights and sounds—a symphony of rustling leaves, the soft padding of woodland creatures, and the gentle murmur of unseen streams that wound their way through the underbrush.

As she ventured deeper into the forest, guided by the map's intricate markings, Ember became keenly aware of a presence watching her—a silent guardian whose eyes were the emerald leaves above and whose voice was the whispering breeze. There were moments when she swore she could hear the ancient trees themselves speaking in hushed tones, their branches swaying in silent conversation as if sharing secrets that had been kept since the dawn of time.

The journey through the forest was not merely a physical passage but a spiritual awakening for Ember. Each step brought her closer to understanding the interconnectedness of all living things and the delicate balance that sustained the enchanted realms. She encountered magical creatures—sprites that flitted through sunbeams like playful spirits, wise old owls that perched atop ancient oaks and shared cryptic wisdom, and elusive face whose laughter echoed through the glades.

Among the dappled shadows and sunlit clearings, Ember found herself unraveling layers of mystery and wonder. The forest seemed to respond to her presence, revealing hidden pathways and sacred groves where ancient rituals had once been performed. She learned to read the language of the woodland—symbols carved into bark, patterns woven into spiderwebs, and the songs of birds that carried messages on the wind.

THE GUARDIAN OF THE WOODS

Days turned into weeks as Ember navigated the labyrinthine paths of the forest, each twist and turn leading her closer to the heart of its mysteries. She encountered creatures of legend—sprites that danced on beams of sunlight, wise old owls whose eyes gleamed with the wisdom of centuries, and elusive face whose laughter echoed through the glades like tinkling bells. Yet amidst the magic that wove through the forest like a shimmering tapestry, Ember sensed a presence watching her—a guardian whose vigilance transcended the passage of time.

One moonlit night, as Ember sat beside a tranquil pool reflecting the stars above, the guardian revealed itself. A creature of ethereal beauty emerged from the shadows—a spirit born of the forest itself, its form shifting between human and animal with each heartbeat. Eyes the color of amber regarded her with a mixture of curiosity and ancient wisdom, a silent acknowledgment of the journey that had brought her to this enchanted realm.

In a voice that echoed with the resonance of wind through ancient boughs, the guardian spoke of a prophecy written in the stars—a tale of destinies intertwined and a future yet to unfold. It spoke of an ancient pact forged between realms unseen, of balance teetering on the edge of chaos, and of a bearer chosen to walk the path of transformation. Ember listened with rapt attention, the words weaving through her mind like threads of a tapestry being spun by unseen hands.

The guardian became Ember's guide and mentor, imparting wisdom that transcended the boundaries of mortal understanding. Together, they delved deeper into the mysteries of the forest, uncovering ancient rites and forgotten lore that spoke of a time when magic flowed freely through the veins of the earth. Through their shared adventures and quiet conversations beneath starlit skies, Ember began to understand the role she was destined to play—a guardian of the balance between light and shadow, protector of the enchanted realms she had come to cherish.

With each passing day, Ember's bond with the guardian deepened, forging a connection that resonated with the harmony of the natural world. Together, they faced challenges that tested Ember's courage and resolve, from confronting ancient spirits bound by oath to deciphering cryptic prophecies hidden within the whispering leaves. Through it all, the guardian stood steadfast by her side, a beacon of strength and wisdom in a world where the boundaries between reality and myth blurred with every step.

THE CLEARING

Guided by the guardian's wisdom, Ember continued her journey deeper into the heart of the forest until she came upon a clearing unlike any she had seen before. Moonlight filtered through the canopy above, casting a silvery glow upon a circle of standing stones that rose from the earth like ancient sentinels guarding the secrets of the land. Their surfaces were etched with runes that shimmered with an ethereal light, each symbol pulsing with a power that resonated deep within Ember's soul.

At the center of the clearing stood an altar hewn from a single block of stone, its surface polished smooth by the passage of time. Runes spiraled outward from its center, forming a pattern that mirrored the constellations above—a celestial map etched into the very fabric of the earth itself. Ember approached the altar with a mixture of awe and reverence, the ancient tome clutched tightly in her hands.

As she laid the tome upon the altar's surface, a surge of energy rippled through the air, causing the runes on the standing stones to glow with an inner light. The forest around her seemed to hold its breath, as if waiting for a revelation to unfold. In that moment, Ember felt a connection to something greater than herself—a thread of destiny woven into the tapestry of her life, binding her to a path that had been set into motion long before she was born.

The stones began to hum with a low, melodic resonance, their ancient runes casting shifting shadows that danced across the clearing. Ember could almost hear the whispers of the past, the voices of those who had come before her, their stories interwoven with the fabric of the land. She reached out, her fingers brushing against the cold, smooth surface of the altar, and felt a surge of memories flood her mind—visions of distant lands, of battles fought and won, of alliances forged in the fires of necessity.

As the runes on the stones glowed brighter, the air around Ember seemed to thicken with magic. She could feel the presence of the forest's spirits, their eyes watching her with a mixture of curiosity and approval. The guardian of the woods, now standing beside her, placed a reassuring hand on her shoulder, its touch grounding her in the reality of the moment.

A soft voice, like the rustling of leaves in a gentle breeze, filled the clearing. It spoke of ancient secrets and timeless truths, of a destiny intertwined with the fate of Eldoria and the enchanted realms beyond. The voice spoke of the ancient pact, of the balance that must be preserved, and of the trials that lay ahead. Ember listened, her heart swelling with a newfound sense of purpose. The journey that had begun with the discovery of the ancient tome was far from over; it was only just beginning.

As the last echoes of the voice faded into the night, Ember knew that she had been chosen for a purpose greater than herself. The clearing, with its ancient stones and celestial map, was a place of power, a nexus of the old world and the new. She stood there, the ancient tome open before her, feeling the weight of the prophecy settle upon her shoulders. The path ahead was fraught with challenges, but Ember knew that she was not alone. With the guardian by her side and the wisdom of the forest to guide her, she was ready to face whatever lay ahead.

ECHOES IN CODE

Amidst the virtual echoes of forgotten code, Alex discovers a hidden server farm—a clandestine sanctuary where the true extent of the conspiracy unfolds. The room hums with the rhythmic pulse of servers, each one holding the encrypted secrets that echo through the corridors of the digital realm.

As he navigates the server farm, the whispers of the past become tangible. Each server, like a vault, contains echoes of projects long thought abandoned and algorithms designed to manipulate the fabric of reality. The conspirators' master plan reveals itself in the intricate dance of data, and Alex senses he is on the brink of exposing the Silicon Conspiracy's core.

Cryptic messages etched in code lead him deeper into the server farm's labyrinth. The echoes resonate with the unspoken language of a hidden agenda, and the room becomes a testament to the conspirators' meticulous orchestration of chaos. The very foundations of the digital world seem to tremble beneath the weight of their sinister designs. Alex uncovers layers of encrypted files that detail the conspirators' plans, each revelation more shocking than the last.

As he unravels the threads of forgotten code, Alex comes face-to-face with the architects of the conspiracy. Shadows of individuals he once considered allies emerge, casting doubt on the authenticity of every line of code. Betrayal echoes through the server farm, mirroring the duplicity that has become synonymous with the Silicon Conspiracy. He realizes that some of these individuals were coerced into their roles, adding complexity to his quest for justice.

Here, the server farm becomes a stage for the final act—a confrontation with the puppet masters pulling the strings. As Alex deciphers the echoes in code, he inches closer to the revelation that will expose the true purpose of the conspiracy and reshape the destiny of technology and humanity. He encounters a former mentor who confesses their involvement under duress, providing critical information that helps Alex piece together the final puzzle.

A climax builds with a showdown in the heart of the server farm. Alex and his allies face off against the conspirators in a battle of wits and code, each side trying to outmaneuver the other. The outcome of this confrontation will determine the future of the digital world and the legacy of those who fought to uncover the truth.

THE REVELATION

Suddenly, a voice echoed through the clearing—a voice that resonated with the wisdom of ages past and the promise of futures yet to come. It spoke of prophecies written in the stars, of a bearer chosen to unlock the mysteries of the enchanted realms and to restore balance to a world on the brink of transformation. The voice carried with it the echoes of ancient tongues, each word imbued with a power that reverberated through Ember's being.

As she listened, Ember's understanding of the journey she had embarked upon deepened. The ancient tome, the map hidden within its pages, and the guardian's guidance through the forest were all threads woven into a tapestry of destiny that had been waiting for her touch. The voice spoke of challenges yet to be faced, of allies to be found in unexpected places, and of a darkness that threatened to engulf both the mortal realm and the realms beyond.

In that moment, Ember's connection to the ancient forces of the forest and the realms beyond became unmistakably clear. The guardian's presence beside her was no longer just a comforting presence; it was a symbol of the unity between the earthly and the mystical, the past and the future. The runes on the stones seemed to pulse with life, their glow intensifying with every word spoken by the unseen voice. Ember felt the ground beneath her feet, the roots of ancient trees, and the heartbeat of the land itself resonating with the ancient prophecy.

The voice continued, weaving a tale of a hero destined to bridge the realms, to fight against the encroaching darkness with the light of knowledge and courage. It spoke of Ember's role as not just a seeker of truth but as a protector of the balance between the worlds. The trials ahead were not merely tests of strength or wit but of heart and spirit, challenging her to grow and evolve with each step.

In her mind's eye, Ember saw visions of the future—battles to be fought, friendships to be forged, and mysteries to be unraveled. She saw herself standing at the forefront of an epic struggle, a beacon of hope in a world threatened by shadows. The ancient tome, now lying open on the altar, seemed to glow with an inner light, its pages turning of their own accord, revealing secrets and spells that would aid her in her quest.

As the revelation washed over her, Ember felt a profound sense of clarity and resolve. The journey was no longer just a path of discovery; it was a sacred mission, a calling that she could not ignore. The guardian of the woods, with its eyes filled with ancient wisdom, nodded in silent affirmation, its presence a constant reminder of the strength and support that surrounded her.

With a deep breath, Ember closed her eyes, absorbing the weight of the prophecy and the promise of the future. She knew that the road ahead would be fraught with danger and uncertainty, but also with the potential for greatness and transformation. The clearing, with its ancient stones and celestial map, was not just a place of power—it was a gateway to her destiny. And with the guardian by her side, she was ready to face whatever challenges lay ahead, knowing that she was not alone in her journey.

THE CALL TO ADVENTURE

With newfound determination burning in her heart, Ember accepted the mantle placed upon her shoulders. She vowed to honor the trust bestowed upon her by the forest's guardians and to embark on a quest that would unravel the mysteries of the enchanted realms. The path ahead was fraught with peril and uncertainty, yet she knew that she could not turn back. The fate of Eldoria and the balance of worlds beyond depended upon her courage and resolve.

Leaving the sacred clearing behind, Ember ventured deeper into the heart of the forest, guided by the map's intricate markings and the echoes of the guardian's words. The path before her twisted and turned through shadowed glens and sun-dappled clearings, each step bringing her closer to the unknown that awaited. Along the way, she encountered beings both strange and wondrous—a tribe of nomadic elves whose songs echoed through the trees, a reclusive sorcerer who dwelled in a tower of shimmering crystal, and a band of mischievous sprites who delighted in leading travelers astray.

Despite the challenges and dangers that lay ahead, Ember found solace in the knowledge that she was not alone in her journey. The guardian of the woods, ever watchful from the shadows, offered guidance and protection when needed most. Its presence was a constant reminder of the interconnectedness of the enchanted realms and the importance of her quest.

As she traversed deeper into the mystical realms, Ember's senses became attuned to the subtle energies that permeated the land. She felt the pulse of ancient magic in the whisper of the wind through the leaves, the shimmer of moonlight on tranquil waters, and the echo of distant voices carried on the breeze. Each encounter with the denizens of the forest—the elves with their age-old wisdom, the sorcerer with his arcane knowledge, and the sprites with their playful mischief—provided clues and insights into the greater tapestry of the enchanted realms.

With each passing day, Ember's confidence grew, tempered by the challenges she faced and the allies she gained along the way. The path was not always clear, and there were moments of doubt and hesitation. Yet with the ancient tome securely tucked beneath her arm and the map as her guide, she pressed onward, driven by a sense of purpose that burned brighter with every step.

In the quiet moments of reflection beneath starlit skies and beside murmuring streams, Ember contemplated the magnitude of her quest. The ancient prophecy, the guardian's guidance, and the bonds forged with allies all pointed toward a destiny that intertwined with the fate of the enchanted realms. She knew that the trials ahead would test not only her strength and skill but also her resolve and compassion.

With the weight of prophecy upon her shoulders and the support of the forest's guardians at her side, Ember embraced the call to adventure with unwavering determination. The journey had become more than a quest for knowledge and power—it was a quest for understanding, unity, and the preservation of balance in a world on the brink of transformation.

THE TRIALS

Each trial that Ember faced tested not only her strength and skill but also her faith in the path she had chosen. In the heart of a labyrinthine maze guarded by riddles and illusions, she confronted her deepest fears and emerged with newfound clarity. Across the treacherous peaks of the Frostspire Mountains, where icy winds howled like vengeful spirits, she forged alliances with unlikely allies who pledged their loyalty to her cause. In the sunken ruins of an ancient city swallowed by the sea, she unearthed artifacts of unimaginable power that spoke of a time when gods walked among mortals.

Yet with each triumph came a greater awareness of the forces arrayed against her—a dark sorcerer who coveted the secrets hidden within the ancient tome, an army of shadowy creatures that sought to extinguish the light of hope, and a malevolent entity whose hunger for power threatened to consume all in its path. Ember knew that her journey was far from over, that the final battle awaited on the horizon where destiny and doom converged.

The trials she faced were not just physical or magical—they were trials of the spirit and tests of character. In the company of her newfound allies—a fellowship forged in the crucible of adversity—Ember discovered strength in unity and courage in the face of overwhelming odds. The bonds she formed with the elves, the sorcerer, and the sprites grew stronger with each shared challenge, each victory against the darkness that threatened to engulf them all.

In the quiet moments between battles, Ember reflected on the lessons learned and the wisdom gained from each trial endured. She found solace in the words of the guardian of the woods, whose guidance had proven invaluable throughout her journey. Its presence remained a constant source of reassurance and inspiration, a reminder of the interconnectedness of all life and the importance of preserving the balance between worlds.

As Ember stood on the precipice of the final trial, her resolve hardened like tempered steel. The ancient tome, now brimming with spells and incantations learned along the way, pulsed with the promise of victory and the weight of responsibility. The path ahead was fraught with peril, yet she knew that she could not falter. The fate of Eldoria and the enchanted realms depended upon her courage and the strength of her allies.

With determination burning in her heart and the echoes of prophecy guiding her steps, Ember prepared herself for the ultimate confrontation. The trials she had faced had prepared her for this moment—the moment when destiny would be decided, and the future of the enchanted realms would hang in the balance.

THE CONVERGENCE

At last, Ember stood upon the precipice of destiny, the ancient tome clutched tightly in her hands. Before her stretched a landscape transformed by the ebb and flow of ages past—a battleground where light and shadow clashed in a symphony of elemental fury. The forces of darkness gathered on one side, their ranks bolstered by fear and despair, while allies from across the enchanted realms stood united at her side. The guardian of the woods, with eyes ablaze with determination, stood shoulder to shoulder with a legion of elves, dwarves, and creatures whose loyalty she had earned through courage and compassion.

As the battle raged around her, Ember felt the weight of prophecy settle upon her shoulders like a mantle of stars. With each incantation spoken, each spell unleashed, she channeled the ancient magic that pulsed through her veins—a legacy passed down through generations, a legacy that bound her to the fate of worlds beyond. Amidst the chaos and fury, she glimpsed the face of her adversary—a dark sorcerer whose eyes gleamed with malice and whose laughter echoed through the tumultuous air.

In a clash of wills and powers that shook the very foundations of reality, Ember and the dark sorcerer engaged in a battle that transcended mortal understanding. Flames of arcane energy surged and clashed, lightning crackled across the battlefield, and the earth itself trembled beneath their feet. Yet in the end, it was not raw power alone that determined the outcome— it was the strength of Ember's heart, the compassion that guided her every action, and the belief in a future where light would always triumph over darkness.

As the final echoes of battle faded into the dawn, Ember stood victorious amidst the ruins of a world forever changed. The dark sorcerer lay defeated, his ambitions shattered like broken glass, while the forces of darkness melted into shadows that dispersed like mist in the morning sun. The enchanted realms, once divided by fear and mistrust, began to heal beneath the light of a new dawn—a dawn heralded by the courage of a young woman who had dared to defy fate and forge her own path.

With the ancient tome returned to its rightful place within the heart of Eldoria's library, Ember Holloway returned to the life she had once known—a life forever touched by the whispers of destiny and the promise of new adventures yet to come.

REFLECTIONS

In the aftermath of the battle, as the enchanted realms began to heal and rebuild, Ember found herself reflecting on the journey that had led her to this moment. The trials and tribulations, the friendships forged and sacrifices made—all had shaped her into the person she had become. With gratitude in her heart and a sense of awe for the power of destiny, she visited each corner of Eldoria, now touched by the renewal that followed the defeat of darkness.

The townsfolk greeted her with a mixture of reverence and relief, their eyes alight with gratitude for her bravery and determination. The bookstore, "Whispers of Eldoria," seemed to hum with a renewed energy, its shelves now adorned with volumes that spoke of triumph and resilience. Ember, with a quiet smile and eyes that held the wisdom of one who had seen beyond the veil of ordinary existence, resumed her role as the heart and soul of the shop. Each morning, she unlocked the heavy oak door, greeted by sunlight filtering through stained-glass windows that now depicted scenes of hope and renewal.

Above the bookstore, in her attic apartment adorned with maps, tapestries, and artifacts collected during her journey, Ember found solace in the quiet moments of reflection. The ancient tome, its pages now filled with notes and memories of the battles fought and victories won, remained a reminder of the interconnectedness of all life and the enduring power of compassion. She often found herself lost in its pages, tracing the journeys of heroes and heroines whose names had faded from memory but whose deeds had shaped the very fabric of history.

In the company of the guardian of the woods, whose presence continued to watch over Eldoria with a silent vigilance, Ember discovered a newfound sense of peace and purpose. Together, they walked through the enchanted forest, now vibrant with life and teeming with stories waiting to be told. The spirits of the land whispered their gratitude, their voices carried on the wind—a testament to the unity forged between mortal and magical realms.

As Ember gazed upon the tranquil streets and mystical depths of Eldoria, she knew that her journey was far from over. The enchanted realms held mysteries yet to be unraveled, adventures yet to be undertaken, and prophecies yet to be fulfilled. With each sunrise that painted the sky in hues of dawn, she embraced the promise of new beginnings and the knowledge that she was forever bound to the tapestry of destiny—a guardian of light in a world where darkness would always seek to test her resolve.

ETERNAL EMBER